Cross Your He

would help us all go below the surface of bullying. Judy helps focus on the impact of our choices on those people around us, helping us realize the deeper levels of our own lives and how we can find inner healing and ultimately redemption regardless of our past. *Cross Your Heart* would be a great read for students and for those who are concerned about the next generation. Get the bullying conversation started with *Cross Your Heart*.

— Jeff Smyth
Coordinator of Community Initiatives Scarborough
Youth Unlimited (TYFC)

Cross Your Heart by Judy Kirwin is an engaging and beautifully written story for children and adults alike. Join 'Kyle' on his 'pilgrim's progress' as he confronts cyber-bullying, guilt, shame and temptation on his way to discovering what true freedom really means. *Cross Your Heart* is a story for our time with a message that is timeless.

— Reverend Canon Kimberley Beard
Senior Priest and Pastor, St. Paul's on-the-Hill Anglican
Church, Pickering, Ontario

Why should teenagers read *Cross your Heart* by Judy Kirwin? Teenagers should read *Cross your Heart* because It reminds teens of the terrible consequences of bullying and specifically cyberbullying. This story would be most intriguing to teenagers because we are so involved in social media. *Cross your Heart* teaches teenagers to be careful and cautious of what we post on the internet. Besides the bullying aspects, this is a well written story that is interesting and will be loved by teenagers and people of all ages.

— Doreen M.
Student

Judy Kirwin

cross your heart

Cross your heart

Scripture quotations marked (NIV) taken from the Holy Bible, New International Version ®, NIV® Copyright © 1973, 1978, 1984, 2011 by Biblica, Inc.® Used by permission. All rights reserved worldwide. Scripture quotations marked (NASB) are taken from the New American Standard Bible®, Copyright © 1960, 1962, 1963, 1968, 1971, 1972, 1973, 1975, 1977, 1995 by The Lockman Foundation. Used by permission. Scripture taken from The Message. Copyright © 1993, 1994, 1995, 1996, 2000, 2001, 2002. Used by permission of NavPress Publishing Group. Scripture quoted by permission. Scripture quotations marked (NET) are taken from the NET Bible® copyright ©1996-2006 by Biblical Studies Press, L.L.C. All rights reserved. Scripture quotations marked (KJV) taken from the Holy Bible, King James Version, which is in the public domain. Scripture quotations marked (NLT) are taken from the Holy Bible, New Living Translation, copyright 1996. Used by permission of Tyndale House Publishers, Inc., Wheaton, Illinois 60189. All rights reserved.

Printed in Canada

ISBN: 978-1-4866-0556-9

Word Alive Press
131 Cordite Road, Winnipeg, MB R3W 1S1
www.wordalivepress.ca

MIX
Paper from
responsible sources
FSC® C016245

Cataloguing in Publication information may be obtained through Library and Archives Canada.

Cross your heart

is dedicated to my husband, Peter, whose
servant heart and sacrifice has made the
writing of this book possible.

acknowledgements

CROSS YOUR HEART HAS CERTAINLY BEEN A TEAM EFFORT AND I would like to thank those who helped me with this project. Much recognition is due to my husband, Peter, who invested his time being its first editor and provided constructive analysis. Special gratitude is extended to my English major son, Kevin, who assisted in writing technicalities. Sincere appreciation goes to my parents, Bruce and Eleanor Doney, who gave advice and feedback. Heartfelt thanks to friends Nicole Chan, Shirley Cua and Darien Krentz who reviewed the story and made practical suggestions as well. Most of all, I'd like to acknowledge Jesus Christ my Saviour, who not only inspires the journey, but is the Author of it all.

Sincerely,
Judy Kirwin

chapter one

IT WAS THE WORST MONDAY AFTERNOON OF HIS FIFTEEN-year-old life. Sitting amongst his peers, Kyle Newman shifted in his seat as he watched his homeroom teacher, Mrs. Donaldson, enter the classroom dabbing her eyes with a Kleenex. The principal followed, looking grim. The usual chatter trailed off into expectant silence.

Despite her emotional state, Mrs. Donaldson tried to regain her composure by straightening the papers on her desk. Six feet tall and dressed in a charcoal grey suit and crisp white blouse, she naturally commanded respect. Her students willingly gave it, for she often went out of her way to help them succeed.

"Mr. White is with me today because I need to tell you some tragic news." She hesitated, then shook her head as fresh tears filled her dark eyes, spilling down her cheeks. "One of your classmates, George Gadde, committed suicide over the weekend. Early police reports point to cyberbullying as the cause."

Ripples of shock and disbelief swept through the classroom, hitting Kyle with full force. He recalled his Facebook message from the night before—a picture of George from swim class. Kyle had thought it hilarious to write the classic rhyme beneath it:

Georgie Porgie puddin' and pie
Kissed the girls and made them cry
When the boys came out to play
Georgie Porgie ran away...

He'd even added the words: "Why George... I don't think you *can* run!"

Well, it certainly wasn't funny now.

Slouching in his chair to avoid the teacher's eyes, Kyle's thoughts raced to justify himself. George had usually laughed right along with them! Somewhat appeased, Kyle ran his fingers through his short spiked blonde hair and glanced at his friend, Mike, whose eyes pointed straight ahead.

A knot formed in his stomach as he listened to what Mr. White was saying.

"We at St. John's High School have zero tolerance for

bullying in any form. It's serious business. George might still be alive today if everyone in this room had taken this message to heart." The principal's deep, authoritative voice stopped abruptly to allow his sharp black eyes to peer over his dark-rimmed glasses. "As part of the investigation, the police told me they need to conduct some interviews with his classmates. That's you guys, so don't be surprised if you're called upon. When we catch the person or people responsible, they will be expelled."

The knot in Kyle's stomach tightened. *I can't be expelled. What would my parents think?*

Mr. White continued relentlessly. "Mrs. Donaldson and I think it would be best if all of you, in addition to your regular homework, write a three-page report on the effects of cyberbullying and hand it in tomorrow. Now, I'm sure the news of George's suicide has come as a shock, and we want to remind you of the grief counselling that is available through the guidance office. Mrs. Dinsdale is specially trained to help you work through this. Do you have any questions?" He waited, eyeing the class carefully. "Well, if not, perhaps some of you would like to speak to us privately. We'll make ourselves available for that if need be."

He gave a short nod to Mrs. Donaldson.

"I expect the cyberbullying report handed in first thing tomorrow morning," she said. "Class dismissed."

The sound of chairs scraping the floor broke the silence as the students stood up, grabbed their backpacks, and started towards the exit.

Kyle was among the first to leave. He hurried down the hall towards the double door exit where his bike was chained up in the schoolyard. He couldn't get out fast enough.

"Hey, Kyle! Wait up!" Mike yelled behind him.

Slowing his pace, Kyle felt agitated even though Mike was his best friend. He looked over his shoulder as Mike jogged up to him.

"What's the rush, man?" Mike punched him on the shoulder playfully. Nothing seemed to bother Mike. It was a trait Kyle envied.

"Got to get home," Kyle mumbled. "Mom wants me to walk the dog." It was a lie; he hoped Mike didn't notice.

The painful subject wasn't addressed until they reached their bicycles.

"I can't believe George is dead. What a loser!" Mike said as he worked through his combination lock. "I mean, what could have been so bad that he took his life?"

Not being able to articulate his mixed emotions, Kyle muttered a quick, "Yeah. I'll see you tomorrow. I gotta run."

As he steered his bike towards home, all he could focus on was removing the incriminating swimsuit picture of George from his Facebook profile.

It was a windy April afternoon, causing Kyle to pedal harder. He lived with his parents in the Beaches, a coveted area for most Torontonians. Oblivious to his beautiful surroundings, Kyle bent over the bike's frame, pedalling into the wind. His legs pumped as he raced down the final steep hill. This was usually the best part of his ride;

speeding past parked cars and feeling the wind whip around his face thrilled him. Hopeful that he would beat yesterday's riding time of fifteen minutes, he pushed even harder.

Upon reaching the bottom, the road veered to the right. Kyle leaned in to the curve, suddenly alarmed to see an oversized trailer loaded with logs right in front of him. He quickly applied the brakes, then panicked to discover they weren't working. The chain had jumped off the rear sprocket.

He had to make a split-second decision. He could squeeze by on the right, risking parked cars, or make a blind pass on the left into the oncoming lane.

As he pulled out to pass, horror gripped him. He had made the wrong decision. He barely had time to register the ten-tonne truck's grill as it smashed into him, driving the handlebars into his chest and crushing his ribs. The truck's chrome bumper launched the bike's frame back towards him, shattering his pelvis and snapping his femur like a dry twig. He was tossed like a ragdoll through the air, then came to land face-first into the pavement.

Kyle didn't know how much time had passed when he heard concerned voices speaking around him. He tried focusing on what they were saying while at the same time straining to open his eyes. They felt like steel-trap doors.

"It looks like he's coming to," a man's voice stated matter-of-factly. "You've been in an accident and it's important to lie still. If you can hear me, look at me..."

With every ounce of strength, Kyle looked in the direction of the voice. The deep voice kept repeating his question, oblivious to his effort.

"Stand back," another man's voice commanded in the distance. "Allow the paramedics to do their work."

As Kyle lay on the cold pavement in agony, he felt a warm breeze brush over his face and chest. It increased in intensity and speed, weaving around his body and seeming to lift him, spiriting him away from the pain and shock of what had just occurred.

Hearing a low-pitch groan, he awoke, startled to discover that the paramedics' blue-green uniforms had transformed into a leafy green, and their brown boots looked like weathered bark. An eerie silence replaced the concerned voices of the crowd; the truck's thick grill now resembled intertwined tree branches.

Worst of all, he was alone. When he got a better look around, he realized the people had all vanished and in their place was a forest.

Where am I? Am I dreaming? Perhaps I'm on some kind of drug?

Taking short breaths in an effort to calm himself, he realized the agonizing pain from just moments before had disappeared. Feeling strange and disoriented, he closed his eyes, hoping that when he reopened them he would return to a familiar place.

The effort was useless. This was not a dream.

Kyle struggled to sit up and was shocked to see that he was no longer wearing the jeans and sweatshirt he'd put on that morning. Instead he wore a dark brown robe, frayed at the knees and arms. Most alarming, however, was the discovery of a heavy chain wrapped around his chest.

Pale grey sunlight poked through the leaves above, its rays falling on slender tree branches. Kyle became anxious upon realizing that those thick branches formed a circular wall that held him captive. There was no way to escape.

Am I in prison? What have I done to deserve this?

chapter two

THE AFTERNOON OF JUNE 12, 1999 WAS A HAPPY ONE FOR Gayle and Josh Newman. It was the day they welcomed their third child into the family. Third, because Gayle's last pregnancy had ended in a miscarriage. Born at 12:32 p.m., they named their new son Kyle Joshua, after his great-grandfather who had famously explored Wales' waterways. Their hope was that he would embody his name's meaning: "narrows, channel, strait." Perhaps he would bring balance into their somewhat chaotic lives. Their strong-willed first son, seven-year-old Keith, was being looked after by his grandparents that day.

"Congratulations," Josh's dad said over the phone when he called with the good news. "Please give our love to Gayle!"

"I sure will, Dad! Is Keith nearby? I'd like to talk with him for a bit."

"Ah yes." His dad hesitated, as if he had been about to say something more but then decided against it. "Keith? Come say hi to your dad. He has some good news for you."

"Hello?" Keith said abruptly.

"Hey Keith," Josh began. "What's new? Are you having fun at your grandparents?"

"No," Keith replied. "It's really boring."

That didn't surprise him, as Keith was difficult to please. Most activities were boring as far as he was concerned, except for sports. He was four feet tall, skinny, and had tousled brown hair, freckles, and brown eyes. His second-grade teacher, Mrs. Sallum, had written in his report card, "Keith is a smart boy. Motivation is key…" Josh and Gayle had always felt like failures when it came to motivating Keith.

"Well, I have some exciting news," Josh announced. "You have a baby brother. His name is Kyle."

Click.

Josh had expected this reaction, but it still came as a shock to hear the dial tone. As he walked back into the hospital room, he tried to keep his emotions in check. He proffered Gayle a bold look so she wouldn't suspect anything.

"Hey, honey," he greeted with a smile. "I told Keith he has a new baby brother. Mom and Dad send their love and they'll probably be here later this evening."

Gayle smiled contentedly and closed her eyes. It had been a long, tough labour.

She awoke to the sound of Keith yelling, "I don't want to go in, Grandpa. No!"

Josh eyed his wife, briefly put his hand over hers in reassurance, then hurried out into the hall. Tears of disappointment welled up in Gayle's eyes at her son's demonstrative refusal to welcome their new family member.

After speaking with Josh in hushed tones, Keith entered the room with a scowl on his face. Wrapped around his hand was a string tied to a blue helium balloon with the words "Welcome to the world, little one" written on it.

"Keith, come and take a look at your baby brother," Gayle urged, pointing to the blue bundle in the crib. "His name is Kyle."

"I already know that! And I don't *like* the name Kyle." Keith sulked, folding his arms.

Josh grabbed the boy's hand and walked over to the crib. Keith turned his face away once he got to the crib, but then out of the corner of his eye he examined his new brother with curiosity. It was an encouraging first step, Gayle thought.

• • •

When Kyle started Kindergarten, Josh and Gayle paid Keith to walk him home from school, feed him a snack, and watch him until one of them got home around 6:00 p.m. "It'll be a bonding experience, you'll see," Josh assured his wife.

One afternoon on their way home, Kyle sprinted eagerly ahead so he could get home to play with his toy race car. In his enthusiasm, he tripped on a sidewalk crack and skinned his knees.

"You are *such* a baby," Keith sneered. "Stop crying! That's what you get for taking off! Get up!"

Although Kyle tried to stop sobbing, persistent tears ran down his cheeks. Limping home, a pain deeper than his scraped knees crept into Kyle's young soul. He learned two important things that day. First, he would get no sympathy from Keith, and second, he had to look out for himself. From that day onwards, Kyle shuddered whenever Keith glared at him from across the table at dinner. Sometimes their mom would notice and scold Keith, but oftentimes she didn't see.

The beating began one day after Kyle returned Keith's model glue. Keith sat at his desk with his back to him. Kyle entered the room and said tentatively to the back of Keith's head, "I've borrowed your glue and now I'm giving it back."

"What did you say?" Keith snapped, turning to face his brother.

Kyle repeated himself, a bit louder this time. "I've borrowed this and I'm giving it back." He held out the glue.

"Who gave you the right to come into *my* room and borrow *my* glue without asking?" Not waiting for an answer, he grabbed Kyle's arm and tore the glue out. He then pushed him down. When Kyle yelled, Keith cupped his hand over his brother's mouth. "Don't yell, *cry baby,*" Keith whispered. "And don't tell Mom and Dad. If you do, you'll be sorry! Cross your heart and swear to me you won't tell them."

Terrified, Kyle nodded, tears spilling down his cheeks.

Tucking Kyle into bed that night, Gayle noticed an unusual sombreness in her son, but she dismissed it, thinking it was due to the lateness of the hour. She hurriedly read a bedtime story. Before turning off the light, she listened to Kyle repeat the same prayer he always prayed. When it came time to say "God bless Mommy and Daddy and God bless Keith," he barely got the words out.

"Is there something you want to tell me, Kyle?" Gayle asked.

"No, Mom," he replied sadly. He had crossed his heart promising he wouldn't tell on Keith, especially with him eavesdropping in the next room.

chapter three

"LEAVE ME ALONE!" KYLE YELLED, WONDERING WHAT HE HAD done to deserve his predicament. He looked into George's phantom face, now floating in the air in front of him. George's piercing eyes held his own. They stared at each other for several minutes. "Why did you take it so seriously? Did you have to kill yourself over it?" This was met with silence. "I'm sorry, all right? It was all a joke!"

Kyle felt a bit better after speaking his peace. To his relief, the face vanished.

I've got to get out of here, he decided in desperation. Utilizing what little movement his chains allowed, he pushed himself up with his elbows and painstakingly felt his way around his woven barrier in the hopes of discovering a hole to push himself through. There were no holes, only cracks between the branches just wide enough for him to see into the forest.

What am I doing here? Kyle asked himself this question over and over, and the same disturbing answer kept repeating itself: *I must be paying for what I've done. I deserve to be in this prison, chained up and alone.* The thought of being alone bothered him the most.

Moving his head close to the slits in the wall of interwoven branches, Kyle cried out again, hoping his voice would be heard.

"Help! Please *help* me!"

Only the sound of the wind came back to him. Pain filled his heart at the thought that he might never see his parents again. Then again, perhaps he didn't want to see them, not after what he'd done. Tears of anguish rolled down his face.

"Please... somebody help me?"

Instead of his wish being granted, a suffocating blanket of silence covered him and he felt an overwhelming urge to doze off. He didn't know if he was dreaming or not when he heard a sinister voice: "It's no use trying to escape, Kyle. You're mine!" An evil laugh punctuated the statement.

A cold sweat broke out on Kyle's forehead. Had he dreamt these words?

He heard the sound of snapping twigs and lifted his head in anticipation, his heart racing. His eyes were drawn to a bright light in the distance. It was coming towards his wooden cage. He didn't know if he should hide or continue crying for help.

Kyle shut his eyes, feeling vulnerable and afraid. Wanting to conquer his fear, he forced his eyes open to get a glimpse of the one who held the light. It was a man, roughly six feet tall, dressed in jeans, with a red and black plaid shirt and a baseball cap that held back wavy, shoulder-length brown hair. The man put the lamp down, took off his backpack, and unclipped a saw hanging from his side. He began cutting through the branches.

chapter four

"MOM?" SIX-YEAR-OLD KYLE ASKED ONE EVENING AS SHE PUT him to bed. "Will the Easter bunny come tonight and hide chocolate eggs everywhere?"

His mom laughed softly. "I wouldn't be surprised, but you know Easter isn't just about chocolate eggs and the Easter bunny."

"It isn't?" Kyle asked, surprised.

"No. It's the celebration of remembering how Jesus, God's Son, died on the cross and came alive again. It's about new life."

"Really? Cross your heart?"

"Of course, honey." She planted a kiss on his forehead. "See you in the morning."

chapter five

NOT KNOWING IF THE STRANGER WAS THERE TO RESCUE OR
hurt him, Kyle anxiously watched the tip of the saw carve an
arch into his fortress. The man removed the branches one
by one, beginning with the top and working his way to the
ground. Grey light filtered in, gradually flooding his cell. Once
the job was done, the man held the lamp before him and
entered Kyle's space.

"Hello, Kyle."

"How do you know my name?" Kyle asked, stunned.

"I know everything about you," his rescuer said,
placing the lamp at Kyle's side. Kyle caught a glimpse of
his rescuer's face as he bent down. His amber eyes were

unlike any Kyle had seen before. There was a calmness about him, too.

He looked down in shame, wondering if this man knew about his role in George's suicide.

"Who are you?" Kyle asked once curiosity forced him to again examine his visitor. "And where did you come from?"

"Name's Clete," he answered. "I came as soon as I heard."

"Heard what?"

Instead of answering, a look of concern crossed Clete's face. "How are you feeling, Kyle?"

"A bit better, but I'm not sure where I am. Can you tell me?"

"Not right now." Clete opened the brown leather bag strapped around his waist and pulled out a green jar. "This will give you the energy you need for the journey ahead."

Clete unscrewed the lid. Because Kyle's wrists were bound, the man held the jar up to Kyle's lips. Kyle greedily gulped down a mouthful of honey water, more of his strength returning with every swallow.

"How do you feel now?" Clete asked as Kyle finished the bottle.

"Pretty good," Kyle said. "What was that stuff, anyway? Some sort of Gatorade, only better?" He thought he should get some for his baseball team. Maybe it would help them win.

Clete smiled and screwed the top back on the jar before placing it in his bag. "It isn't available where you come from." He studied Kyle's face for a moment. "My assignment is to accompany you to see the King. He sent me to get you. We need to go. He's waiting for us."

The King... expecting me? A sudden fear gripped Kyle. *Why would a king want to see me?*

"Do you have enough strength to stand?" Clete asked.

"I'm not sure," Kyle replied, recalling the embarrassing fact that his wrists were bound and his chest laden with a heavy chain. "Clete, I think I will need your help."

Clete reached out his hands, grabbed hold of Kyle's outstretched bound wrists, and pulled him up. Once on his feet, Kyle turned his attention towards the lantern, whose light shone on his wrists to determine what actually held them. He saw that they were shackled together with a short, thin chain. Instinctively, he tried pulling his wrists apart, but it only resulted in a clanging sound and pain in his joints. A thicker chain encircled his chest like a tangled root. The semi-darkness revealed nothing else.

He was helplessly trapped.

Looking at Clete, he saw in his amber eyes a comfort and peace that lent him courage.

"I'm not exactly sure what these chains are about," Kyle remarked. "I know I didn't have them before I got here."

"You'll find out soon enough." Clete handed him a walking stick, then led the way with his lantern held aloft. "We don't have far to go."

They passed through the archway the man had cut earlier and Kyle breathed easier. He was leaving his prison behind.

As Kyle followed Clete, his thoughts were pulled back towards his part in what had happened to George. Fear crept into his heart and his head hung low. *I wonder if the King will know what I did. How can I escape a king's judgment?*

Without warning, he heard a thud and felt something heavy land on his head.

"Hey! What's going on?"

To his horror, a huge black spider dropped down in front of his face, its beady eyes holding his for a second before swinging to his chest and spinning him into a cocoon. Kyle struggled to free himself from the beast's clutches, but the more he tried, the more ensnared he became. Crawling up his chest with its eight spindly legs with lobster-like pinchers, the creature went for Kyle's throat.

"Clete! Help!" Kyle cried, finding his voice.

Clete looked over his shoulder, ran back to him, and pointed at the terrifying insect. "Be gone, creature of darkness!"

The massive spider fell backwards and scurried into the trees.

Shaken by his brush with death, Kyle wondered who this man was whose words had such power. Clete reached for the hunting knife clipped to his belt and began carefully slicing away the silken threads around his chest.

"Kyle, you must forget what is behind you," Clete instructed firmly. "Press on. You need to maintain this mindset, or something far worse will happen."

Once free from his threaded tomb, Kyle asked, "What do you mean?" Clete faced him with a look of amusement—and waited. In a flash of insight, Kyle answered his own question. "Is there some sort of connection between what I thought and what happened to me with that creature-thing...?"

Clete nodded.

chapter six

KYLE AWOKE TO EASTER MORNING, ONE OF TWO SUNDAYS A year on which the Newman household attended Richdale Community Church, where his grandparents were long-standing members.

"Kyle, hurry up and get dressed," his mom called from the kitchen. "We'll be leaving in half an hour."

"Okay, Mom, I'll be right there." Kyle yawned and jumped out of bed. He pulled his favourite baseball shirt over his head and stepped into his black pants.

When he entered the kitchen, his dad looked up from his newspaper, coffee cup in hand. "Good morning, sleepy head!" he teased, grinning at his younger son.

Keith, focused on his cereal, didn't acknowledge him. As Kyle sat down at the table, his mom placed a bowl of cereal in front of him and kissed his forehead.

"Have a good sleep?" she asked. Still attractive at thirty-five, Gayle had maintained her athletic physique by religiously attending a weekly swimming class at the local community centre. She wore a purple blouse with matching scarf and a short black skirt and hose. With her blonde hair swept up, she looked especially beautiful.

"Yeah," Kyle replied. He hurriedly ate his cereal and gulped down a glass of orange juice, thinking all the while about their upcoming trip to church. Over the years, Kyle hadn't minded going to Kingdom Kids; the meetings were so different from going to school. The teacher, Mrs. Johnston, always seemed delighted to see him, even though there were at least twenty other children in the room.

At church, he learned more about the God he prayed to at bedtime. He remembered hearing about how God was strong and loved him enough to send His Son to die for the wrong things he did. God had conquered death, too, and if he believed he would live forever. Somehow this didn't make sense. *If He's so powerful, how come my brother is so mean to me, even though I ask God to make him stop?*

chapter seven

ALTHOUGH CLETE HAD TOLD HIM TO FORGET WHAT WAS behind him, Kyle still had to fight a feeling of apprehension with every step he took towards their destination. He was puzzled over the thought of this king, and what might be expected of him.

Who am I that the King would want to see me? he asked himself repeatedly while looking down at the chain wrapped around his dark, tattered robe.

"Clete?" Kyle asked, feeling self-conscious. "Do you think I could get cleaned up a bit before visiting the King?"

Clete peered over his shoulder and waited until Kyle caught up. "No need to be concerned, Kyle. The King doesn't mind what you look like. In fact, he can't wait to see you."

Kyle shook his head in disbelief, shame piercing his heart as he again thought about George's suicide. Somewhere nearby, a creature of darkness shrieked, a reminder for him to press on and not lag behind.

Sunlight streamed through the trees, finally allowing Clete to lower his lantern. He clipped it to the side of his backpack.

They continued along a stony path leading to a clearing with a beautiful garden. Clusters of roses in a rainbow of colours had been arranged around several ponds with high fountains. Kyle, who had never paid much attention to gardens before, couldn't help but be taken aback by its splendour and the sweet fragrance in the air.

Beyond the garden emerged a beautiful palace made of amethysts, emeralds, and rubies. It was unlike anything Kyle had ever seen before. The colourful gems captured the sunlight and reflected their exquisite beauty.

"Awesome!" Kyle remarked. "This sure is better than the castles I've seen in pictures."

Clete laughed. "Come, Kyle."

He motioned for Kyle to cross the narrow bridge that led to a golden gate, the entrance to the King's palace. As they made their way over the bridge, Kyle's eyes were drawn to the words carved in stone above the gate: "All are welcome."

Kyle stood at the threshold of the palace's open doors, noticing a golden staircase ascend in front of them, its banisters sparkling with rare gems. Upon looking to his left, he saw a long corridor ending with slightly parted doors. To his right gleamed a ballroom with marble floors, white walls, and floor-to-ceiling windows. The room's lovely chandeliers sparkled with thousands of diamonds.

"Kyle?" Clete pulled him back from his reverie. "This way."

Clete pointed towards the doors, which were also fashioned from gold. Together, they stepped onto a red carpet. As they neared the doors, they began to open wider. A brilliant, inviting light radiated through the crack.

chapter eight

SUMMER WAS A FAVOURITE TIME OF YEAR FOR TEN-YEAR-old Kyle. No teachers. No school. Sleeping in. Playing baseball. Spending two weeks at his grandparents' cottage in the Muskokas was a definite highlight. It had been a family tradition ever since he was a baby. There, his grandpa had taught him how to build a campfire, and how to swim and canoe. He loved the water and spent most of his time near it.

"Kyle, I think you've reached the age that you can canoe by yourself," his grandpa told him one morning after breakfast as they walked down the pathway that led from the cottage to the lake.

"Really?" Kyle asked eagerly, his mind racing ahead, thinking of what an adventure it would be to take the canoe out by himself.

Grandpa didn't answer right away, but when they reached the dock he handed a life jacket to Kyle. "Why don't you head for Cedar Point and take Snickers along for company?"

Snickers, a chocolate-coloured lab, followed Kyle everywhere, so it didn't take much convincing for her to jump into the faded blue canoe.

"Awesome!" Kyle yelled enthusiastically as he stepped into the canoe and reached for the paddle on the dock.

"Hey, don't forget to put that life jacket on," his grandpa said, reaching down and taking hold of his baseball cap; he gave it a tug for emphasis. "You'll need it. Remember, the squalls come up pretty quick around the bend. You'll have to keep your wits about you. I'm sure you'll be fine, though, because you and I have braved those waters before and we never had a problem."

Kyle loved how his grandpa instinctively knew how to encourage him to be a man, not like his parents, who tended to indulge their youngest son.

"Yeah, yeah," Kyle said absently as he struggled to tie the laces of the life jacket.

"Okay, it looks like you're ready to go now," Grandpa said, throwing the ropes into the canoe and giving it a slight push.

Kyle smiled broadly as he dipped his paddle into the water, inching the canoe forward. "Thanks, Grandpa!"

Soon he was paddling with greater confidence. Snickers moved to the front of the old canoe, sniffing the air and looking intently at the shore for any sign of wildlife to give her an excuse to bark. With every stroke of the paddle, Kyle felt more certain he could conquer any wave that came his way.

The water was calm as he passed near the point. Seagulls flew overhead, their white bodies standing out against the pale blue sky. The sound of water lapping against the canoe relaxed him so much that he didn't notice right away when its intensity changed. The wind picked up, driving the water into turmoil. It didn't seem to matter that Kyle paddled harder. The waves restrained him. Sensing danger, Snickers barked wildly.

Without warning, a powerful whitecap caught them broadside, overturning the canoe and sending Kyle and Snickers plunging into the cold water. Instinctively, Snickers began swimming towards the shoreline.

The shock of finding himself in the water made Kyle's heart race. *Where's the paddle?* He saw it a couple of waves away and swam towards it as best he could with his life jacket on. Grabbing it, he returned to the overturned canoe and held onto it with his free hand. He then kicked his legs as hard as he could to move the canoe towards the shore, but the wind and waves were too strong.

Shall I let the canoe and paddle go? Take off my life jacket? If I do, I can swim towards the beach more easily.

It was tempting. He looked towards shore and saw that Snickers had almost reached it.

Should I or shouldn't I? And then Kyle found his answer. *No. Grandpa said to always stay with the boat and not to even think about taking off the life jacket!*

Snickers stepped onto the land, shaking herself dry. She turned her attention towards Kyle, barking as if trying to encourage him to follow her.

Frustrated at his inability to move towards shore, Kyle once again pulled the canoe with his left hand. In his right, he clutched the paddle. A cool wind whipped at his face and wet hair, causing him to shiver. After only five minutes of being tossed by the waves and struggling to hold on, Kyle felt exhausted. It was only the life jacket that kept his head above water now. Good thing he was determined to follow the safety rules.

His thoughts began to wander. For some reason, Kyle remembered Mrs. Johnson, the teacher at Kingdom Kids, telling him that God sees all and would help him if he asked.

"God... are You there?" he began tentatively. "I know I haven't talked with You much, but I could really use Your help now. If You wouldn't mind helping me, I'd really like that. Please... please help... help me!"

He waited. The sound of the wind and crashing water mocked his request. His heart sank, but he wasn't surprised. Why would God help him? He hadn't before, so why would He now?

It was then that Mr. Brown, a cottager, saw the dog barking on his beach. As he got closer, he realized it was his friend's dog, Snickers.

That's odd. What's she doing here?

He approached to pat her head, but Snickers paid no heed. Mr. Brown followed her lead and soon saw the overturned canoe and a person bobbing up and down in the water. Could that be Kyle?

"Hold on!" Mr. Brown called at the top of his lungs. "I'm coming!"

Kyle saw Mr. Brown waving his arms at him and felt relieved. *I've been seen.* With great effort, he held fast to the canoe and waited to be rescued.

Snickers jumped into the old man's rowboat, eager for another chance to get to Kyle. As they neared him, she barked happily.

"Kyle, are you hurt?" Mr. Brown asked.

"No." Kyle felt dejected. "I just couldn't swim and push the canoe at the same time."

"Of course you couldn't. That's too tough when the waves are like this. Here, give the paddle to me. Good. Now loop this rope through the handle at the front of the canoe and give it back to me so we can tow it back to shore."

Kyle looped the rope through the handle and swam awkwardly to pass the rope to Mr. Brown. He tried pulling himself into the boat, but he was too worn out.

"Here," Mr. Brown said, offering his hand. "Grab on to me and I'll pull you in."

Kyle readily took the man's extended hand. With the waves pushing against them, Kyle lost his grip and slipped back into the water.

"Sorry, Kyle, let me try again," Mr. Brown said with determination.

Kyle pulled himself up with one arm and the old man tugged on the other. Soon Kyle got his stomach atop the boat's rail. With one more heave, he finally flopped down into the boat. Snickers licked his face in greeting.

"Thanks, Mr. Brown." Kyle looked up into the man's wrinkled, weather-beaten face.

"I'm glad you're safe! We'll take you back to your grandpa's." With that, Mr. Brown began rowing as hard as he could with the canoe in tow.

Kyle shivered uncontrollably. Noticing, Mr. Brown took off his sweatshirt and handed it to him. Kyle put it on, but he couldn't shake the feeling that he had failed to handle this situation by himself. He felt ashamed to face his grandpa.

chapter nine

CLETE PUSHED OPEN THE GOLDEN DOORS. KYLE HESITATED before following him.

"Are you sure the King wants to see me?" Kyle whispered as loudly as he dared. "Perhaps you were supposed to rescue someone else. Maybe you got us mixed up."

"Kyle, I don't make those kinds of mistakes. You are the one the King is expecting, and I don't want to keep him waiting any longer."

Upon hearing those words, Kyle followed him into the room with confidence. Once entering, a sense of overwhelming love and acceptance greeted him. He hadn't experienced these emotions in such a profound way before. His eyes couldn't stop filling with tears.

"Welcome, Kyle, I've been expecting you," spoke a deep, gentle voice from within the light. "Come."

Although drawn to the warmth of the voice, Kyle became aware of the heaviness of his chains. For an instant, he felt an urge to run away. Clete, sensing his hesitation, placed his hand on Kyle's back to encourage him forward.

As Kyle stepped closer to the light, the King became visible. Dressed in a floor-length purple robe, he wore a simple golden crown and his arms were outstretched.

Confused, Kyle fell to his knees and looked up into the King's face, strangely captivated by the kindness reflected in his eyes. The longer he gazed, the more he became conscious of his inner shame and guilt. He hung his head. *Perhaps the King doesn't know about what I did to George. If he knew, he wouldn't greet me this way.*

At that very moment, the King reached down and lifted Kyle's chin. "Kyle," he said quietly, "I know about George."

Kyle could hardly breathe as he waited to hear his punishment.

Instead the King asked, "Would you like to be free of your chains, Kyle?"

"Ye-e-es," Kyle stammered, puzzled by the King's interest in him.

"Good. *Very* good. Would you like to know why the chains are there?"

"Yes, Your Majesty. I'm not sure how I got them." Kyle revelled in the fact that one so important knew his name and cared about him.

The light surrounding the King's face seemed to shine brighter. "You need to know what they are, Kyle, in order to be free of them."

With that, the King placed his hand on the chain around Kyle's chest. He lifted it enough for Kyle to see a word written on it: "GUILT." Then the King revealed a word on the shackles around Kyle's wrists: "SHAME."

"What does this mean?" Kyle asked hesitantly. "I'm not sure I understand—"

"Guilt is for the wrong things you've done in your life, Kyle, and shame is the feeling you have about who you are. Your enemy would like to keep you wrapped in these chains." The King paused to let these words sink in. "But that's not my plan for you, my son."

Kyle's head jolted upwards in disbelief. Had he really just called him "my son"? As he looked into the light of the King's face, he felt loved. An inexplicable peace filled his body.

Then a strange thing happened. As he believed that the King's words were true, that he really was his son, the chain of shame loosened its grip around his wrists and clattered to the floor. The sound echoed throughout the room.

Wow! Kyle thought. *My thoughts are really powerful here.*

The King began to laugh, genuinely delighted at Kyle's discovery. "What about the chain around your chest, Kyle? Would you like to be free of that as well?"

"Yes, I would," Kyle replied, thinking it would be as easy as the first.

"There's only one way to be free from your guilt, Kyle. You must go on a difficult journey, but it will be rewarding in many respects. You will learn how to be free from guilt and fear, living your life the way it was intended to be lived. The lessons learned in your travels are up to you." The King eyed him, stirring up the same feelings in Kyle that his grandpa had stirred up years ago when he'd challenged him to be a man. "Are you willing to take the challenge?"

"Yes," Kyle said without hesitation. "Can Clete come, too?"

No sooner had the words left his lips than the King clapped his hands with delight. In a quiet voice just loud enough for Kyle to hear, the King said, "I love your simple trust. This journey will require everything of you. I will supply you with the equipment you need. And yes, of course, Clete will accompany you."

The King sat down on his throne and clapped his hands again. A servant boy dressed entirely in white appeared, holding a velvet square pillow with a black leather book in its centre.

The King handed the book to Kyle. "Open it."

As he did, the pages began to glow and Kyle saw a reflection of himself. Alarmed, he dropped the book as if it was on fire.

"What is this?" he whispered as he bent over to pick it up.

"It's your guidebook," the King explained. "It will light your way and reveal where you are at any given moment. Kyle, where did you see yourself when you looked in that book?"

"I saw a reflection of myself, standing in this very throne room," he answered.

"Right. Now open it again."

As Kyle obeyed and opened the guidebook, he once again saw himself in the throne room, but this time he noticed a heart-shaped stone appear on his chest in the image. It was very dark.

"What is that?" Kyle asked, pointing to it.

"A monitor revealing your heart's condition. Not your physical heart, mind you, but the real you. Remember that the enemy wants to keep your heart the way it is, but my plan is to restore it. As you go on this venture, you'll see this symbol of your heart change according to the choices you make and the words you speak, for it is out of the heart that words are formed and spoken. Guard your heart, Kyle, by being attentive to these heart changes. Now, take a look at the last page of the book and you'll discover where you're going."

Intrigued, Kyle flipped through the pages and stopped at the last one. He recognized a map, but one unlike the paper versions he was used to, this one was alive with colour. Different regions of the map were coloured differently. A path threaded its way through a green forest, blue seas, a yellow beach, a red orchard, an orange tunnel, brown plains, and purple mountain ranges. The colours mesmerized him, and then he noticed all the tiny gold stars sprinkled across the map. He looked at the King quizzically.

"The gold stars mark your arrival in each region," the King said. "You'll also need these."

The King handed him a backpack, along with the walking stick Clete had given him earlier. Kyle took them and noticed a slim button on the walking stick's side. Curious, he pressed it; immediately a pointed steel blade emerged from the end of the stick. It was a sword! He swung it back and forth, aiming it at imaginary enemies. He thought of his best friend, Mike. He'd sure be impressed if he could only see him now.

"The sword is powerful," the King said, interrupting his musing. "It will ward off your enemies as you enter the battlefield. Be alert, for their goal is to keep you in chains."

Kyle lowered the sword uneasily at the mention of the enemies.

The King reached for his arm and held it. "Don't be afraid, Kyle. Remember that you have Clete with you. Be strong! Be courageous!"

His words had a way of inspiring Kyle. Excitement began to build in his heart.

The King walked toward the hallway, with Clete and Kyle falling into step beside him. When they reached the tall golden doors, the King grasped the handle. He smiled at Kyle, reassuring him.

"Look." The King paused as he opened the door. "Your first test is ahead of you."

chapter ten

KYLE'S THIRTEENTH BIRTHDAY STOOD OUT AS ONE OF HIS best. It was the day Keith left home! The whole family was eating birthday cake around the kitchen table when Keith abruptly stood up and announced to their parents, "You both love Kyle more than you love me!"

"Sit down, Keith," Dad instructed. "It's Kyle's birthday. What do you mean, we love Kyle more than you?"

"It's obvious! What did I get for my thirteenth birthday? A lousy sweater and, oh yeah, a bicycle. What does Kyle get? In addition to a bicycle, you gave him a cell phone with a plan that *you* pay for!"

"Keith," Mom began, then stopped, thinking through what she had been about to say.

Dad interjected. "Just because Kyle is given a cell phone doesn't mean we love him more. Don't forget we bought you that car!"

"Yeah, but I have to pay for the insurance," Keith muttered under his breath. "I bet you'll buy Kyle a car someday and pay for his insurance, too! I've had it up to here." He motioned towards his neck. He stomped from the room and several minutes later emerged with packed bags. "I've already decided that I'm moving out."

"Not like this, Keith," Mom pleaded.

They all followed him to his car to say goodbye and were shocked to discover that the car was already loaded up with some of his things.

"Where are you going?" Dad asked.

Keith glared at his father without answering, then got in the driver's seat, slammed the door, and drove off.

In the days that followed, a noticeable change occurred in the Newman household. With Keith gone, Kyle felt as though a weight had been lifted off his shoulders. No more snide remarks, cutting criticism, or sarcasm.

• • •

Later that year, Kyle met his friend Mike. Athletic, good-looking, and popular, Mike was an important guy to be associated with.

One day after school, the two boys saw George walking by himself towards the baseball diamond at the far end of the schoolyard.

"Hey," Mike said to Kyle, pointing in George's direction. "Let's have some fun."

Kyle pulled out his cell phone to text George, but before he did Mike grabbed his phone away and began typing a message. He laughed and then showed Kyle what he had written: *Georgie Porgie, did you have enough lunch?* At roughly two hundred pounds and 5'4", it was an obvious dig. Although Kyle had conflicted feelings about the text, he nodded his approval. Mike pressed send.

After George read the text, he began to laugh and texted back. *Yes, can't you tell?*

The answer surprised Kyle, so he thought he would add to the joke. He wrote back, *Sure can.*

It was the beginning of text putdowns that slowly made Kyle feel a sense of power he had not known before. He began to like it.

chapter eleven

KYLE SAW TWO GATED ROADS ACROSS THE BRIDGE. ONE RAN straight ahead, whereas the other turned sharply to the left. The noise from the road to his left attracted him first. It was wide, paved, and upon it stood lots of people laughing and having fun. There were carnival rides, movie screens, loud music, sports cars, and bright lights. At its entrance, a young man dressed in a white robe called to him: "Hey, Kyle! Why don't you join us?" The voice sounded vaguely familiar.

Kyle began walking toward the teenager, wanting to find out who he was. He soon broke into a run. "Mike, is that you...?"

As he neared the large gate, the face of Mike changed into a stranger's.

"Oh." Kyle blinked. "I thought you were my friend."

The young man laughed. "My name is Mr. Fall Guy. Choose this way and you'll have all these and more..." He held up a backpack overflowing with iPads, iPhones, video games, and money. He then motioned to a Planet X bicycle lying on the ground next to him. Kyle felt drawn to the expensive bike and backpack. He considered how all these tools could help him in his travels.

Mr. Fall Guy put down the backpack and picked up the bike. "It's yours. All you need to do is come with me," he urged. "This is only the beginning!"

As Kyle considered this, he found himself distracted by the rave music. He walked closer to the edge of the road and looked off into the distance. Crowds covered the road as far as he could see, and with them came even more noise, music, lights, and food.

"Where does this road end?" Kyle asked.

Mr. Fall Guy shrugged. "Why does it matter? You'll have a great time getting there! Well, what are you waiting for?"

Feeling uneasy, Kyle turned his face away and looked toward the road to his right. It ran straight ahead. A woman stood at its entrance, her long flaxen hair making her look angelic. She held an antique stopwatch and a handful of shining gold coins. In stark contrast, on either side of this road grew green grass scattered with daisies, submitting themselves to the breeze. The road narrowed and led to a dark forest.

When the woman saw Kyle looking in her direction, she spoke. "Kyle, if you listen to me you will be safe and secure, without fear of evil."

The words didn't make sense, yet deep inside he felt himself drawn towards her. He glanced sideways at Clete, who stood tall and silent beside him.

"Which road are you going to choose, Kyle?" Clete asked, finally breaking the silence.

"Uh, I'm not sure. How can I know which one is right?" Kyle then remembered his guidebook. He pulled it out of his backpack and opened it eagerly. On the page, he saw a reflection of himself at the end of the palace bridge. He took note of the heart symbol; instead of darkness, light now shone through it via small pinholes.

I wonder what that means?

As he gazed intently into the book, the following words appeared: *"Let your eyes look straight ahead... do not swerve to the right or the left..."*[1]

He reread the first part slowly, then looked up and saw the road with the woman whose words had stirred him. He made his decision.

"I must take the grassy road, Clete." When Kyle spoke these words, the paved road and crowds faded into the background.

The woman with flaxen hair stepped towards him, holding out the stopwatch and gold coins. She placed these in his outstretched hands.

"The stopwatch represents long life," she said, "and the gold coins symbolize riches and honour."

---

[1] Proverbs 4:25, 27 (NIV).

Her eyes seemed to read his very soul. Kyle felt self-conscious and decided to put the gifts into his backpack.

"My name is Lady Wisdom," she said in a strong voice, her blue eyes twinkling. "You may not understand yet how significant it is that you chose this road. This is the King's favourite pathway. You passed the first test. Continue straight ahead and do not turn to the left or the right. In this land, believing is the key to moving forward and the way to guard your heart." She moved closer and whispered into his ear: "On this road, you will meet the One you are to believe in."

Her words sent shivers up and down his spine. He nodded as he took the words in, though he didn't fully understand their meaning.

She motioned for both him and Clete to pass onto the road. As they passed, Kyle studied the map at the back of his guidebook, remembering that the golden stars symbolized the regions he would visit. His first destination was a valley in the forest. He examined the road ahead and saw that it led straight into the dark, intimidating woods. Easing his backpack over his shoulders, he pressed on, taking comfort in Clete's strong presence.

As they neared the woods, Kyle decided to press the button on his walking stick, just to make sure it would turn into a sword like it had in the throne room. He felt reassured when it did. When he pressed the button a second time, it transformed back into a simple walking stick.

Up close, the dense forest looked even more uninviting. Thick branches squeezed right to the edge of the path. Twigs scratched at his arms as he progressed into the darkening woods. The scene reminded him of the prison he had been trapped in when he first arrived in this land.

"Do you know of any shortcuts?" Kyle asked hopefully.

"No shortcuts," Clete answered.

Kyle tried in vain to calm his racing heart. "I'm afraid," he admitted. "It's dark and I don't know how to get to my destination."

As soon as he said this, the guidebook lit up in his hand. Gripping it, Kyle held the book out ahead of him. The darkness scattered enough for them to move confidently along the stony path.

"I wish I could see farther down the trail," Kyle said, as the light only made it possible to see a few feet ahead of them. A slight wind rustled the leaves around them. A dog barked in the distance, alerting Kyle to some unseen danger.

As they walked along, Kyle noticed an area that wasn't so dark. The trees had been replaced with tall cathedrals, statues, crucifixes, and various other religious symbols. The lights here were dim, but perhaps better than nothing.

"Look, Clete!" Kyle exclaimed. "See this light? Who would have thought they'd be in a forest? I don't even need my guidebook now." He turned his back on Clete and didn't listen to his words of warning.

I'll make it fine by myself, he thought as he left the path and walked amidst the statues. In his haste, Kyle stepped in what he thought was a mud puddle. This dark substance wasted no time swallowing his feet and working its way up his legs. In his confusion, Kyle dropped the guidebook and watched helplessly as it quickly disappeared into the muck.

chapter twelve

ONE NIGHT IN FEBRUARY, TWO MONTHS EARLIER, THE PHONE rang and Kyle answered. "May I speak with Mrs. Newman, please?" a lady asked.

"Sure," Kyle said. "I'll get her for you."

Not long into the conversation, Kyle realized it was George's mom. Curious, Kyle was able to eavesdrop from the next room even though the TV was turned on. His mom's voice sounded concerned and empathetic.

"Yes, Mrs. Gadde, I'll speak with him." Following the receiver's click, true to her word, Gayle called him into the kitchen.

Kyle dreaded having to be reprimanded.

"Kyle, are you picking on George?" she asked, a look of sadness in her eyes.

"No, Mom," he lied. He didn't want to disappoint her. "Mike and I are only texting him and kidding around. George laughs. He laughs at what we text him. Honest!"

chapter thirteen

"GREAT," KYLE MUTTERED AS HE TRIED UNSUCCESSFULLY to pull himself out of the mire. "Clete! Help me... please help me!"

Kyle looked around frantically. Where was Clete? Hearing some shuffling noises behind him, he turned. In the dim light, he could no longer see the path.

"Clete, is that you?" he spoke into the darkness. The cathedrals and statues had vanished, seemingly transforming into the ordinary bark of this impenetrable forest's dusky trees.

The shuffling stopped. Confused at the silence, Kyle began to brainstorm solutions to his growing problem.

Perhaps he could pull himself out with the help of a tree branch. He felt around with his hands, searching for something to hold onto. He was about to give up when he felt a slimy branch.

"It's worth a try," he told himself. He gripped the branch with all his strength and pulled. He couldn't budge.

Out of the darkness, he heard a stranger's voice calling to him. "It seems to me you need some help. Here, take my hand and I'll pull you out."

Kyle saw the faint outline of a hand extended before him.

"Thank you," Kyle said with relief. As he reached out, however, his hand passed through the air where the stranger's arm should have been. Despite what he could see, there was nothing there.

Is this a figment of my imagination? Why can't I feel it? What's going on?

The stranger's helpful tone turned accusatory. "You're not gripping my hand hard enough!"

"I'm trying as hard as I can!" Even as Kyle said this, a familiar feeling of panic rose in his chest, causing the chain around him to tighten.

"No, you're not," the stranger insisted gruffly. "If you were, I'd be able to pull you out without any trouble."

Kyle looked down at the thick mud clinging to his knees and once again tried moving his legs. He only sank deeper from the effort. He looked at the stranger, dressed in jeans, a sweatshirt, and a black leather jacket.

"What's your name?" Kyle asked.

"Why does that matter?" The man sounded annoyed. "I'm trying to help you, aren't I? Do you want my help or not? Are you going to take my hand?"

Kyle hesitated, catching a faint light shining up from his muddy prison.

It's my guidebook, he realized. He thrust his hand into the cool mud, feeling around until his fingers wrapped around the book. He pulled it up with all his strength. Amazingly, the book still gleamed brightly.

"How is a book going to help you now?" the man sneered. "It's of no use. No use! If you want to get out of the mud, the only way is to put the book down and take hold of my hand."

"I need this book!"

The man's countenance darkened. "Listen, kid, that book won't help you. Think about it. Do books pull people out of mud? No! Come on now, think! Think!"

"Clete!" Kyle shouted into the darkness. "Clete, I need you!"

"Why are you calling for Clete?" the man asked fearfully, looking over his shoulder. "He left you, remember? The only one around is me and I'm offering to help. Why won't you take my hand?"

"I... don't... want... *your*... help!" Kyle spat each word.

"Very well then." The man relented, shaking his head slowly. He turned his back to saunter off into the inky blackness. As he did, Kyle saw the word "RELIGIOUS" glowing on the back of his leather jacket.

He lifted the guidebook as far above the mud trap as he could and tossed it up onto the ground where it would be safe, but this only caused him to lose his balance. He fell back into the muck.

"Ahhhh!" Kyle cried out in desperation. The more he struggled, the more the chain and mud worked together to suck him greedily into the depths. For the second time since he had arrived in this land, tears of frustration spilled down his cheeks.

What am I going to do?

chapter fourteen

A POLICEMAN RANG THE DOORBELL. WHEN GAYLE OPENED
the door, he said, "Are you the mother of Kyle Newman?"

"Yes." Gayle braced herself for the worst.

She had noticed a change in Kyle ever since he'd started
hanging out with Mike. He was more distant from both Josh
and herself, and somewhat disrespectful. Perhaps Kyle was in
some sort of legal trouble. Could it be drugs?

"There's been an accident..."

She listened in disbelief as he informed her that her son had
been hit by a truck and was at that moment being rushed to
Metropolitan General in serious condition. As the words sunk in,
she placed her hand over her mouth and began to wail.

"Are you sure? It can't be..."

The look on the policeman's face convinced her otherwise. "I'm sorry, ma'am."

Hands shaking, she called Josh at work, telling him to meet her at the hospital's emergency department.

chapter fifteen

KYLE TRIED TO SHAKE OFF THE CLOAK OF HELPLESSNESS THAT settled over his shoulders.

"Embrace it, Kyle," a familiar woman's voice urged from the surrounding darkness. "Embrace your helpless feeling. It's the beginning of your freedom."

Startled, Kyle looked in the direction of the voice. Lady Wisdom stepped out of the darkness and stood at the edge of the mud trap. Her outstretched arm pointed upwards. Kyle followed with his eyes and saw that she was pointing towards a tree branch over the muck. It was within his reach! How had he not seen it before?

He stretched out his arms and took hold of the branch, then pulled on it with all his strength. Surprisingly, the muck released him without much of a struggle. He manoeuvred himself around the thick branch, astonished that the limb held his weight so easily. Then he saw a word carved in the trunk. The light from his guidebook shone from the ground, its glow just bright enough for him to make out the word: "CURSED."

Great, Kyle thought, *I'm sitting in a tree that's cursed!*

He peered over to where Lady Wisdom had stood, but she had disappeared. Chills tingled up and down Kyle's spine as he tried to piece the puzzle together. His eyes found the guidebook, whose light also illuminated a wooden sign poking up from the edge of the mud. The word "LAW" had been etched in black on its worn plank.

The more he strained to see through the dim light, the more details he was able to make out. Ten dirt tracks led out from the mud trap like spokes of a wheel, and each track was marked by a wooden spike driven into the ground. These spikes, too, had words carved into them:

Keep the King first.
Worship no others in His place.
Honour Him.
Set one day apart for rest.
Respect your parents.
Don't kill anybody.
Don't betray your love.

Don't take what isn't yours.
Don't tell lies.
Don't set your heart on anything that isn't yours.

All these sentences seemed vaguely familiar to Kyle.

The chain around his chest tightened as he thought of his texts to George. As these memories passed over him, he pictured himself wrestling with someone in the muddy hub of this wheel, but he couldn't see the face of the one with whom he wrestled. Before he caught sight of the person, in the corner of his eye he became aware that Clete was watching the fight from the edge of the mud.

"Clete," Kyle spoke hesitantly.

Clete didn't reply. Instead he grabbed hold of his walking stick and pointed towards the wooden sign with the word "LAW" written on it. As he pointed, another word appeared overtop it, but Kyle couldn't make out the new word until Clete stepped aside. When he did, Kyle observed that it was the same word he had seen on the tree: "CURSED."

Upon making this realization, he saw the face of the one he was fighting: it was himself! The scene quickly faded from view.

"Kyle, do you understand what you just saw?" Clete asked.

"Not really." Kyle shook his head, nestling into the thick branches of the tree. "I mean, how can the law be cursed? Aren't those good principles to live by?"

"Have you ever struggled to obey these laws?"

"Well, yeah." He looked over the ten phrases again. "Take the 'don't kill anybody' one, for example. I didn't kill George, but my words led him to... to..." Kyle choked, the chain around his chest tightening.

...to kill himself, he finished in his own head.

"No one can obey these laws perfectly, Kyle," Clete said quietly.

"Is that why the law is cursed?"

Clete nodded.

Kyle brushed the back of his hand against his cheek to wipe away a tear. "Clete, where did you go when I fell into the mud?"

"I was with you."

"But I didn't see you!"

Clete smiled. "Just because you didn't see me doesn't mean I wasn't there."

Once again, Kyle's attention turned towards the trunk of the tree in which he sat. The word "CURSED" etched into its bark puzzled him the most.

"I don't get it," Kyle said. "Why is this tree cursed? It just rescued me out of that horrible muck."

Then his eyes caught sight of his guidebook, still glowing brightly from the ground. Clete leaned down to pick it up, then handed it to him. Kyle flipped open the page that shone the brightest, and there he saw an image of himself covered in mud. Encouragingly, his heart symbol had grown even more pinholes of light. As he stared intently at the page, words began to appear: *"Cursed is everyone who hangs on a tree."*[2]

 After reading these words aloud, Kyle looked quizzically at Clete. "I don't see anyone hanging on this tree."

[2] Galatians 3:13 (NASB).

chapter sixteen

GAYLE AND JOSH HAD JUST FINISHED THEIR BREAKFAST THE day after the accident, and were getting themselves ready to go to the hospital, when they heard a knock at the door.

"I'll get it," Josh told his wife.

When he opened the door, he was shocked to see a tall police officer holding a search warrant.

"What's this all about?" Josh asked as Gayle joined him in the doorway.

"You've probably heard that one of Kyle's classmates, George Gadde, committed suicide over the weekend," the officer began. "Cyberbullying is the probable cause, and we need to identify your son's involvement."

"I don't believe my son was involved. He's a good kid and has never been in any kind of trouble." He paused, letting out a sigh of resignation. "However, you're welcome to come in and get what you need."

chapter seventeen

"I DON'T SEE ANYONE HANGING ON THIS TREE," KYLE REPEATED.
As soon as he expressed this, a dark veil tore through the air
in front of him and he saw a vision. In it was the same tree,
and pinned to its trunk was a man covered in blood.

Kyle gasped.

"The Powerful One is going to save you, Kyle," Clete said.

Is this bloody man the "Powerful One"? Kyle wondered.
*It just doesn't make sense. If he's so powerful, why doesn't he
save himself?*

The dying man moved his head to look at Kyle, his
compassionate eyes strangely familiar.

Where have I seen those eyes before?

"Come," Clete said. He grabbed hold of Kyle and helped him down from the tree. It felt good to stand on solid ground again.

He looked back up to find the vision still shimmering in the air. His eyes again locked with the man fastened to the tree.

The vision changed, its shocking scenes playing out right in front of him. First, he saw himself in the same wrestling match he had observed earlier. In the next scene, he had his cell phone in hand, fingers moving furiously over its keys. He knew intuitively that he was in the midst of bullying George. The last scene horrified him the most: in it, he saw George's true reaction as he read the disparaging text messages. Kyle could hardly breathe as the chain of guilt squeezed his upper body.

Kyle doubled over, crying as he grasped the chain, trying to pull it from his chest. No matter what he did, it only tightened. Dropping to his knees, he began to weep.

"I'm so guilty," he sobbed. "Is there any hope for me?"

He felt a hand on his shoulder and glancing up to see Clete, whose full attention was aimed at the vision of the man hanging on the tree. As this man looked down, he cried out with great effort, "Father King, forgive Kyle, as I forgive him."

Kyle let these words sink deep within him, and as he did he felt himself bathed in a bright, warm light.

"Into your hands, Father King, I commit myself," the Powerful One said as he drew his last breath.

Darkness crept over them from the surrounding forest and covered the vision until it went black. The air was oppressive, almost too thick to breathe. Kyle detected a light pushing the darkness away and encircling the foot of the tree they stood around.

A new sign had appeared on the trunk, reading: *"When he was hung on the tree, he took upon himself the curse for our wrongdoing."*[3]

"But I don't get it," Kyle said, puzzled and upset. "Why is he the one who had to die? I deserve to be cursed, not him."

"He *is* love, Kyle," Clete said quietly. "He loves you. That's why. He doesn't want you to have to experience the punishment you deserve. It's the only way you can be free. Believe it."

"I do believe." Kyle let himself slowly digest that statement.

For the first time, he noticed a key hanging on a nail just below the new sign.

"That's the key." Clete took the key, then bent down to turn it in the lock of Kyle's chain. Immediately it fell to the ground. With the constriction gone, Kyle was able to breathe easily again. Warm light embraced him as he looked down and saw that his brown robe had vanished, replaced by a clean white one.

"I'm free!" he shouted. "I'm free at last!"

Somebody screamed from the depths of the forest. Remembering Lady Wisdom's instruction, he determined not

[3] Galatians 3:13 (NLT, paraphrased).

to look to the left or right. Instead he gazed up at the tree, amazed to again see the scene of him texting George. The Powerful One's image was superimposed over it, his blood trickling through the memory and causing it to evaporate before Kyle's very eyes.

For the second time, unexplainable peace flowed into his heart where once had resided horror and guilt.

Kyle looked down at the heavy chain at his feet. A star-shaped light gleamed up from the ground. His first destination! Realizing this, he opened the guidebook to the page where it shone brightest and read: *"Your life is a journey you must travel with a deep consciousness of the King. It cost him plenty to get you out of that dead-end, empty-headed life..."*[4] Double-checking the front of the guidebook, Kyle saw that a bright light had completely replaced the darkness around the heart symbol. He showed it to Clete in excitement.

"Yes." Clete nodded, smiling. "It is the Powerful One's doing! Now that you're free from your chains, the King has some gifts for you, including a protective vest to cover your heart. Remember his warning, though: you have an enemy who wants to put you back in those chains."

Clete reached into his backpack, pulling out a vest, helmet, shoes, and belt. He took off a shield clipped to the outside of his pack.

As he handed them over to Kyle, Clete said, "Now you can be ready to fight at any moment."

---

[4] 1 Peter 1:18 (The Message, paraphrased).

Thanking him, Kyle slipped the vest over his exposed chest, dropped the helmet over his head, tied up the new shoes (which fit perfectly), and strapped the belt around his waist. After clipping the shield to his backpack, he felt like a soldier. A new man.

He opened his guidebook to discover his next destination. As usual, an image appeared, this time in the form of a lit path that threaded its way out of the forest toward a vast sea. The next gold star appeared to shine up from beneath the waters.

Clete helped him back toward the grassy path, which pointed the way through the forest. Together, they walked along the path again. As they proceeded, Kyle had an uneasy feeling that many eyes watched them from the shadows.

"Let's go, Clete," Kyle said, wanting to hurry up. "There's water ahead!"

Excited, he broke into a run, forgetting momentarily about his troubled sensation that they weren't alone. Without the heavy chain weighing him down, he felt weightless. He ran along the stony path, hearing Clete's footsteps behind him.

"We're almost there, Clete!"

Kyle spared a glance over his shoulder to make sure Clete was still with him, then turned back to see ahead of him. Sure enough, there was an opening in the forest, and beyond it lay a beach.

Before he could react, arrows flew through the air, splitting the wood in the trees beside him.

"Whaa...?" Kyle dove behind a huge rock next to the path. "What's going on?"

Clete dropped down next to him. "Get your shield in front of you, face your enemies, and stand out there! You're not alone."

"Okay. I don't understand, but I'll do it."

Kyle unhooked his shield from his backpack and hefted it in front of him. He bravely stood up, heart pounding wildly.

"Hey, there he is!" a deep voice called from somewhere in the forest.

A fresh onslaught of arrows poured out from the dense trees. Kyle lifted his shield and the arrows bounced off it. He sat back down behind the rock and picked up one of the fallen arrows. Carved in its head were the words "Do it yourself." As he touched the arrow, smoothing his thumb over the point, four men came into sight. They all wore cool leather jackets. He heard them whispering to each other, but he couldn't make out what they were saying.

"This guy is a pretty good soldier."

"Think of all the arrows we shot, and none hit him."

"We could use him on our team. Maybe we could grab an arrow and pierce his skin to make him one of us."

"I've got a better idea," the fourth man said. He appeared to be the leader. Approaching Kyle in a friendly manner, he asked, "Hey kid, what's that you're holding?"

"An arrow." Kyle eyed the sinister-looking man. He was dressed in black from head to toe.

"Where did you get it?"

"Someone shot it at me."

"That's terrible! Can I have a look?"

Kyle handed over the arrow.

"This isn't a bad arrow," the leader said dismissively. "It won't hurt you. In fact, it will give you incredible power! It'll give you the freedom to do things your way. Your vest, though, has to go. It's too restricting. Take it off and try on this leather jacket." He pulled off his jacket and held it out. "See if it fits."

"No, I'm not taking off my vest," Kyle said evenly. "The King gave it to me, and I belong to the King."

When the four men heard this, they all took a step back.

"Oh," the leader said in a sarcastic tone. He glanced back at his companions. "The King gave it to him. Did you hear that?"

The men sneered at Kyle and began to shout at him.

"Special, eh?"

"You think you're somebody special?"

"You're not special!"

Kyle was alarmed to see these words take physical form, pouring out of the strangers' mouths and transforming into darts. He brought up his shield to protect his face from the onslaught. As he looked down, he saw some of the darts hit his vest and bounce harmlessly to the ground. Their impact jerked him backwards.

Words sure have power!

"Hey, leave me alone!" Kyle said with all the authority he could muster.

The four men started to laugh.

"Scared, eh?" said their leader. "I can sense it. You're afraid."

His heart pounding, Kyle grabbed his walking stick, pressed the button, and pointed his sword. "I believe in the King because I'm his son. He makes me *strong*."

Rays of light beamed from the sword's tip, forcing the archers to drop their bows and arrows and cover their eyes.

Clete placed his hand on Kyle's back. "Good words!" he said. "Now, let's go. We must hurry."

Running down the path towards the sea, they noticed a woman by the water's edge. She was dressed in a flowing white gown.

Is that Lady Wisdom? Kyle wondered.

"Come!" she called to them, her hands cupped around her mouth. "Come quickly. They aren't far behind you."

Kyle glanced behind him to see a thick grey cloud encompassing his enemies. He felt a familiar sense of fear settle around him, trying to trip him up.

As his enemies sprinted in their direction, Clete reminded him, "Don't forget to use your sword!"

Kyle waved his sword at his enemies. Once they saw it, they fell back, giving Clete and Kyle more time to reach the woman on the beach.

As they approached, Kyle jerked his head back in surprise. This woman had the look of his mom in her younger years.

"Mom, is that you?"

chapter eighteen

"MR. AND MRS. NEWMAN?" THE NURSE ASKED, ADDRESSING
Josh and Gayle as they sat by their son's bedside in the
intensive care ward. When they looked her way, she stepped
aside to make way for a policeman. "This is Constable Cook.
He wants to meet with you both. The Quiet Room down the
hall is available for your use."

Josh stood up, and Gayle followed his lead.

Officer Cook shook their hands and then wordlessly
walked with them down the hall towards this so-called Quiet
Room.

They stepped inside and saw that the room was painted
a dusty rose colour. Josh and Gayle settled into comfortable

wing armchairs while Officer Cook closed the door behind him.

Realizing their discomfort, he sat down and tried to put them at ease. "I'm sorry to hear about Kyle's accident. How is he doing?"

"He's been given a fifty percent chance of survival," Josh said with a lump in his throat. "We should know more in twenty-four hours. Now, is there something we can help you with?"

"Yes." The policeman paused. "Perhaps this isn't the best time, but I need to make you aware that as soon as your son recovers, I'll have to ask him some questions. Over the last few days, we've been examining George's online activities. I'm sorry to be the one to break this to you, but Kyle was one of the last to interact with him."

After hearing that news, Gayle let out a soft cry. Josh put a protective arm around her shoulder.

"I don't believe it," Josh said, slowly shaking his head.

chapter nineteen

"MOM, IS THAT YOU?"

Before Kyle's eyes, the woman's face transformed into Lady Wisdom's. "Hurry and catch up to the Powerful One," her gentle voice urged. "He's made a way through the sea for you. Just follow the path."

"Wait," Kyle said. "Didn't I just see the Powerful One die?"

"He didn't stay dead," Lady Wisdom explained. "He has power over death!"

With one hand, she pointed towards the sea, and with the other hand she reached for the sky, bringing down a thick wall of clouds to confuse their pursuers.

The path they had been following now proceeded into the sea, with walls of water rising up on either side. It reminded him of the story of Moses, when God had parted the Red Sea in order for the children of Israel to be led safely through the dry seabed, away from the pursuing Egyptian charioteers.

He examined the path and found that this sand was dry, too.

In the distance, right in the middle of the path, he made out the silhouette of a man. Was it the Powerful One? His heart yearned to catch up with him, to thank him. Because of his sacrifice, Kyle no longer wore his chain of guilt.

Kyle ran along the sandy path, only slowing down when he was halfway to the silhouette.

With a start, he realized what he was doing. His mind flashed back to the canoe ordeal. As the memory washed over him, the walls of water threatened to collapse. He felt splashes of saltwater against his skin and stopped dead in his tracks, feeling terrified. Although an athlete, he hadn't won any medals for swimming!

"Believe in the Powerful One!" Clete called from behind him.

"I do believe," Kyle said weakly.

"Then continue to move forward."

Kyle took another step and the water inched back. Ahead, the silhouette turned and Kyle saw that it was, indeed, the Powerful One. The man smiled, obviously waiting for Kyle to catch up. On his back, the man carried a heavy backpack.

Encouraged, Kyle once again broke into a run.

"Welcome, Kyle," the Powerful One said as Kyle approached.

Kyle smiled, amazed to see the wounds in the man's wrists and feet. "You're the one I saw on that cursed tree back in the woods, aren't you?" he blurted out, already knowing the answer.

"Yes, I am." The Powerful One shifted the weight of his backpack, moving it to a more comfortable position. "I'm going to the deepest part of the sea to get rid of this. Would you like to come with me?"

"No thanks. I want to get out of here. I'm scared!" Kyle was stunned to admit that his fear would hold him back from any sort of adventure. He reconsidered. "Er, well, on second thought, I've made it this far with you. I should be okay."

They started walking together. Kyle observed that the load on the Powerful One's back was huge, and he wondered if he should offer to carry it.

"Kyle, this is something only I can do," the Powerful One said in answer to the unspoken question. "Do you want to know what's in this pack?"

"Yes, I do."

"It's everything that causes division between us. It's what stops us from having a friendship. It's all the bad stuff you've ever said, thought, or done. I'm about to bury it all." He suddenly stopped, the wall of water towering around them. "Here is the place."

The Powerful One placed the load on the ground, then produced a shovel from the side of the pack. Swiftly and easily, he began digging a hole. Strong emotions welled up within Kyle as he considered the significance of what was happening.

At that moment, the same four enemies who had chased Kyle down to the beach arrived.

"What are you doing?" they screeched in unison, amplifying their terror.

With dismay, Kyle saw that they carried the chain of guilt that had once been wrapped around his chest.

"You're not really going to get rid of Kyle's guilt," the leader said. "What you have done is *useless!*"

The Powerful One ignored their accusations as he dug the hole deeper. He dropped the huge backpack into it and then started to bury it. As the men continued to mock him, he stood up.

"Be silent!" As the Powerful One said this, his words transformed into a huge sword. It sliced through the air, targeting the men and striking them down.

"That was amazing!" Kyle exclaimed. He looked up into the Powerful One's face with awe and respect. The Powerful One smiled at Kyle, then stooped over to continue burying the backpack. Soon the hole was completely filled.

Next, the Powerful One gathered rocks from the seafloor. One of them had words written on it which Kyle couldn't distinguish. Nonetheless, Kyle felt a sense of wonder and relief. He needed to pinch himself, in an effort to remind himself where he was—in the depths of the sea! He gazed up at the walls of seawater on either side, much taller than skyscrapers. In those depths, Kyle could see all sorts of colourful fish swimming up to the wall. It was a peaceful moment. He felt surprisingly safe, all things considered. Even so, as he looked up he saw that the sky had turned cloudy and dark.

The Powerful One watched him intently. "Come, it's important that you understand something."

Kyle moved closer, until he stood upon the spot where the pack had been buried. The Powerful One pointed to a stone resting at his feet—the same stone with the writing on it. Kyle now read the words silently: "Here lies Kyle."

"What? I... I don't understand," Kyle stammered. He instinctively moved his hand towards the stone marker, a cold dread gripping him on the inside. "I'm dead?"

"Yes." The Powerful One nodded slowly, his kind eyes holding Kyle's. "Do you remember what I buried beneath this stone?"

"Uh, all the wrong things I've ever done?"

"That's right. Do you understand now? That part of you has died, and now you are a new person, Kyle. This is a cause for celebration!"

As Kyle pondered what this meant, Clete caught up with them. He approached the Powerful One with his hands clasped together. When he opened them, a butterfly rose into the air beating its wings together, its breathtaking colours of orange, gold, and vibrant blue captivating them.

"It wasn't long ago that this butterfly broke out of its cocoon," the Powerful One explained. "This is a picture of what happened to you, Kyle. Now you are free! *Believe it!*"

The butterfly flapped its wings quicker, becoming airborne.

chapter twenty

"I JUST DON'T BELIEVE IT!" JOSH TOLD HIS WIFE AS THEY walked back to their son's room after the meeting with Officer Cook. "How could Kyle do something like that? Where did I go wrong?"

"Don't blame yourself, Josh," Gayle said. "What Kyle chooses to do is up to Kyle."

They rounded the last corner toward his room when Gayle stopped short.

"What's the matter?" Josh asked.

"Shhhh."

Gayle pointed to the nurses station. To Josh's surprise, he saw Keith talking with a nurse. They hadn't seen or spoken with their oldest son since he'd left two years before, though they had tried to reach him several times. Now here he was, a few feet away.

They looked at each other as if to ask, *How did he find out about Kyle?* Dressed in black jeans and a leather jacket, the only noted difference in their son was shoulder-length hair pulled back in a ponytail.

Gayle's eyes welled up.

"Well, well, well. This should be interesting," Josh commented, giving his wife a Kleenex.

As they walked towards the nurses station, Keith turned and faced them. "Mom... Dad." He gave them both a short nod in greeting. "How is he?"

Gayle couldn't hold back her cries.

Josh put a protective arm around his wife. "We'll know better tomorrow. Let's go into his room where there's a bit more privacy."

"If it's all the same to you, I'd like to go alone. I need some one-on-one time with him."

Josh frowned, puzzled by his son's request. "Sure, okay by me. Gayle?"

"Okay by me, too," Gayle said, her mascara running.

"Uh, Keith?" Josh said.

"Yeah?" he answered, eyeing his dad warily.

"Thanks for coming."

Keith entered the room alone. Seeing his brother in such a critical state shocked him to the core. Standing over him, he said nothing for several minutes. Then the words spilled out: "Kyle, you're a jerk, but I was a jerk, too, and I'm sorry for being one. If you pull through this, I'll make it up to you. Maybe things can be different. Maybe we can change. After all, Mom and Dad need you. Do you hear me?" He put his lips right to Kyle's ear and repeated himself. "Mom and Dad need you."

Machines beeped rhythmically at the head of Kyle's bed in response.

A gentle knock at the door caused Keith to turn just as a nurse entered.

"You'll have to excuse me," she said. "It's time to change Kyle's bandages."

Afterward, Keith found his parents in the waiting area sipping hot drinks. His dad stood up as he approached.

"It's good to see you, Keith," Josh started, trying to bridge the years of silence. "We've missed you. You're welcome to stay as long as you want."

chapter twenty-one

THE POWERFUL ONE TOUCHED KYLE'S SHOULDER WITH HIS scarred hand, and Kyle once again looked into the eyes of the one who had made him new.

Kyle's attention was then drawn to a star-shaped rock on the path just ahead. It lit up, and he saw that he had again reached a destination! He walked towards the star and read the words carved on it: *"You must display a new nature because you are a new person..."*[5]

Both Clete and the Powerful One observed attentively as Kyle reflected on the words before him.

---

[5] Ephesians 4:24 (NLT).

"A new person?" Kyle asked, looking up. "Impossible. I can't do that. There's no way!"

Grinning, the Powerful One agreed. "You're right. Remember this: *'my power is made perfect in your weakness.'*[6] I'm the One who's doing something new in your life. Trust me."

Something about him made Kyle feel safe, so he blurted out everything that caused him the most pain. "What about George? I did something terrible. I wrote and said words to him that led him to commit suicide. He's dead because of me."

Kyle looked down, too ashamed to meet the Powerful One's searching eyes. Surprised, he saw the Powerful One's feet move towards him and felt the man's fingers under his chin, lifting it up.

"Kyle, I know all about this," he said, looking into his tear-filled eyes. "I don't condemn you. I've buried it here, remember? The old Kyle, and all his ways, is buried here, too. What will the new Kyle be like? My way is not to tear people down; it is to build them up. It is not to use cutting words, even if you think it's all a joke; it is to affirm and encourage others. People are valuable and everyone has a special purpose."

"I'm so sorry for the words I used in my texts to George," Kyle said. "I want to choose your way, I really do. When I came to this land, I was bound up in chains. Then the King

---

[6] 2 Corinthians 12:9 (NIV).

told me that my chains were called guilt and shame. They were horrible. When I learned that I was the King's son, my shame was unlocked. The key to unlock my guilt was found on that cursed tree where you took my punishment."

The Powerful One nodded. "Guilt and shame have no power over you now, Kyle, because you believe in me and belong to the King. You are forgiven. I know that you're sorry for the words you said to George. Choose to walk in your freedom and don't return to your chains."

The three began moving again towards the far shoreline, where Kyle noticed a flicker of light. As they emerged from out of the sea, he could tell it was a small fire. Two figures stood next to it. As Kyle, Clete, and the Powerful One drew near, Kyle noticed that both were young women dressed in white with golden sashes around their waists. One held a bottle of ointment, and the other, a dagger.

They were so similar in appearance that Kyle thought they might be twins. Lovely auburn hair flowed down their backs. Their jubilant faces gazed upon the Powerful One.

"Mercy is the one holding the ointment, and Truth holds the dagger," the Powerful One explained. "They'll come to your aid when the phantom chains of guilt, fear, and shame try to recapture you. Mercy and Truth overcome guilt, fear, and shame. "

"I don't understand. How will they know to come to my aid? What do I need to do?"

"You worry, yet there is no need to. Trust me, Kyle. *Trust* me. Just ask for my help and they will be there."

Kyle turned his attention to the young women. Their clear green eyes sparkled as they smiled in unison. They didn't seem very strong, but he was beginning to trust the words of the Powerful One.

Again, the Powerful One touched Kyle's shoulder and motioned for him to follow. As Kyle did so, Clete and the Powerful One walked on. They left the beach and walked towards the grassy hills beyond. Birds flew overhead and swooped towards them. The air was fresh and clear and the sun shone brightly.

Kyle suddenly realized he was hungry. It wasn't the gnawing hunger he was used to. Rather, he longed for the *taste* of food. Past the hills, they came upon a grove of fruit trees—apple, orange, banana, and mango. The fruit looked so scrumptious from afar that he ran ahead without waiting for his travelling companions or telling them what he was about to do.

With the chain gone, it felt good to run and feel the wind on his face. The trees were farther than he thought, but finally he reached an apple tree. Eagerly, he reached out and took hold of an apple. He tugged at it, expecting it to release itself from the branch. Instead, the apple resisted. Kyle kept pulling, and finally it let go—only to immediately wither in his hand!

chapter twenty-two

THE HOURS DRAGGED. THE STRAIN OF THE LAST COUPLE OF days was beginning to wear on both Josh and Gayle, and it showed on their faces. Lack of sleep, nervousness, and practically living in the waiting room proved difficult.

The intensive care nurse assigned to Kyle knocked on the door before entering. "Mr. and Mrs. Newman?"

"Yes?" Josh said.

"There's someone at the nurses station who's here to see Kyle. He seems upset and I wonder if one of you could come and speak to him."

"I'll go." Josh stood up and stretched his arms over his head, yawning quietly. He followed the nurse out.

To his surprise, Kyle's friend Mike sat in the waiting area.

"Hey, Mike!" Josh said, encouraged that a friend of Kyle's would come and visit. He sat beside the boy. "The nurse says you're upset. Anything I can do to help?"

"Just how bad is Kyle, anyway? I've heard stories at school and I want to find out what's going on. Is he going to die?"

Josh hung his head. "We don't know, Mike, we just don't know. We're hoping he'll pull through. He's got a fifty percent chance."

Mike jerked his head back in surprise. "Fifty percent? That's all?"

"Do you want to see him?"

"Uh, I just can't. I can't face it right now. There's too much going on in my own life for me to deal with this."

"Oh?"

"Yeah."

Knowing that Mike's dad had been killed in a car accident five year before, Josh took on a fatherly role. "Do you want to talk about it?"

"I'm in trouble. The police are investigating me over George's suicide," Mike confided. "Tomorrow I'll be interviewed by one of the investigators and I'm scared."

"Tell me about that," Josh said, hoping to gain insight through Mike about his own son's involvement.

"First off, you need to understand that we were only joking around. George laughed at our text messages. We didn't mean anything by them."

"We?"

"Kyle and me."

"Go on."

"I just can't shake this feeling of guilt whenever I think of George. I can't believe he's dead."

chapter twenty-three

KYLE DROPPED THE WITHERED FRUIT, THEN STOOD BACK TO examine the tree. It looked like a normal, healthy tree, yet there was something odd about it. The bark was smooth to the touch—not weathered and rough like the apple trees back home. Its leaves were green, yet upon closer examination he saw they were filled with tiny holes as if something had been consuming them from the inside-out.

Then Kyle noticed that beneath the tree rested a shining star—another destination point. He pulled his guidebook from his backpack, thumbing to the page that was lit up, where he read, *"Be wise as serpents and innocent as doves."*[7]

---

[7] Matthew 10:16 (NET).

Hmmm. That sounds like some kind of warning!

Just then, a man dressed in a woollen coat and hat appeared from behind the trees. He had fleecy white hair and beard that reminded Kyle of Santa Claus.

"Hello, young man!" he said cheerfully. "Hungry, are you? Well, what would you like? I'll get it for you. How about a mango? Or perhaps a banana?"

Taken aback, Kyle replied, "Ah, that's okay. I don't think this fruit is any good. I just picked an apple and it withered in my hand."

"I saw that," the woolly man said, shaking his head back and forth sympathetically. "It's because *I* didn't pick it for you. I'm the keeper of the fruit trees and they only respond to my touch."

The trees respond only to his touch? How could that be? Kyle looked behind him to discover the whereabouts of Clete and the Powerful One, but the keeper of the trees blocked his view.

"Well, which one would you like?" the man persisted. "Why are you taking so long to decide?"

Kyle's appetite waned as he peered into the old man's eyes. There was a darkness there that made him feel uneasy.

"Here, look." The man's eyebrows rose pointedly as he took a banana from the tree beside him, peeled it, and took bite after bite, chewing noisily. "Don't you want to have one? It's delicious!"

Kyle believed him and his desire began to grow for a small taste. It had been so long since he'd eaten.

Maybe it would be good to have one, he thought. The strange man picked a banana and handed it to him. As soon as he felt the banana in his hand, to Kyle's utter disbelief, the man's nose elongated, his blue eyes turned brown, his snowy hair turned black, the coat fell off him, and he dropped to all fours. Claws replaced his fingers. Kyle's eyes widened and a gasp escaped his lips. The man before him had transformed into a huge, snarling wolf!

Paralyzed with fear, Kyle screamed, "*Help!*"

The wolf lunged towards his throat as Kyle closed his eyes, protecting his face with his arms.

Before feeling the claws rip into his shoulders, however, he became aware of another presence. Bright light squeezed through the cracks of his eyelids. He heard a sharp yelp, followed by silence. Daring to open his eyes, he saw the Powerful One before him, with the wolf's head under his foot, its eyes lifeless.

"What *was* that? How could that old man change into a wolf?" Kyle asked, heart pounding. "I thought I was done for sure. I couldn't bear to look!"

"There are many who seek to entice and lead you away from me," the Powerful One explained. "They are wolves in sheep's clothing. As for the fruit, come to my table. All you have to do is ask."

"Then I'm asking for some fruit."

As Kyle looked around the grove, he noticed a table set out beyond the trees. He hurried to the table and plucked up a banana from a silver platter.

"This fruit is awesome," Kyle said. "It's the best I've ever tasted!"

Thinking again of his close call with death, he saw Lady Wisdom appear and begin to speak with the Powerful One. He recalled her words at the start of his journey along the narrow road. She had said, "He who listens to me will be safe from evil."

Why didn't I listen? Kyle thought. *How could I have been so stupid as to run ahead and nearly die over a piece of fruit?*

He looked down and noticed, to his horror, the outline of a chain growing back around his chest. *What? No! It can't be...*

But it was. The chain of guilt was reappearing.

"The chain is growing back!" Kyle cried out in disbelief. "Powerful One? Please help me!"

Suddenly, both Mercy and Truth appeared before him. Truth reached for her dagger and cut the chain, saying, *"There is therefore now no condemnation..."*[8] Mercy poured her ointment on his fast-beating heart, which calmed under her gentle touch. Mercy smiled reassuringly and echoed her companion's words, "There is no condemnation," and added, "for those who believe in the Powerful One."

Kyle became aware that the Powerful One was watching, his gaze unwavering. "Truth always sets you free, Kyle. That's its very nature."

Mercy and Truth took each other's hands and slowly walked back towards the beach.

---

[8] Romans 8:1 (NET).

Unexpectedly, Kyle noticed another star nailed on a fencepost near one of the fruit trees. It flickered, beckoning Kyle to come and read its message: *"The truth will set you free!"*[9] Kyle picked up the star from its post and put it in his backpack. The guidebook glowed in response. It was a good reminder, just in case the chain of guilt ever began to re-emerge.

Still shaken by his near-death experience and the proud heart that had led to it, Kyle looked up into the Powerful One's face in awe. Not only had this man died to forgive all wrongs and take away Kyle's own guilt and fear, he had also rescued him from the jaws of the wolf.

"Why did you do this?" Kyle asked, his eyes brimming with tears. "Am I really that valuable to you?"

Love shone out from the Powerful One's eyes. With his arms outstretched, he leaned in to give Kyle a hug. An overwhelming sense of peace came over him.

Lady Wisdom touched his arm. "Trust your heart to the Powerful One," she said. "Cross your heart and tell me you will. This is the only wise choice. Don't trust your own heart without him."

Kyle nodded in agreement, a lump in his throat.

"You must continue on with your journey," the Powerful One said. Then he made a promise. "I'll meet you on the other side of the tunnel."

Turning, the Powerful One and Lady Wisdom walked on ahead.

---

[9] John 8:32 (NET).

With the open guidebook in hand, his backpack on, and Clete by his side, Kyle looked down at the book's page and saw an image of himself standing by the fruit trees; his heart symbol glowed brightly. The intensity surprised him, because he didn't feel he deserved this. He had let the Powerful One down.

As soon as this thought entered his mind, an arrow whizzed by. The enemy was near!

Kyle untied his shield from his backpack. With his shield in front of him, he consulted the guidebook again. It indicated that he was to head towards a wide, broad plain. He looked straight ahead, matching the landscape with what he saw in the map. A wide path proceeded before him, gradually becoming narrower. On both sides of the path, rounded walls rose up, resembling a long tunnel.

This must be the tunnel the Powerful One told me about.

Small windows opened into the sides of the tunnel. People watched him from those windows. He couldn't get a good look at their faces, for whenever he glanced in their direction, they withdrew. Uneasiness crept into his heart.

His guidebook began to emit pulses of light. Opening it, Kyle saw himself at the entrance. Next to it was a message: *"When I am afraid, I will trust in you... I will not be afraid. What can mortal men do to me?"*[10]

He turned to Clete. "I'm ready. Let's go!"

As they stepped into the tunnel, Kyle brandished his sword and shield, ready for battle. It wasn't long before he

[10] Psalm 56:3–4 (NIV).

heard the sound of rushing wind; another arrow sped by, landing in the ground two feet away.

On the arrow, there was a note.

"Walk on," Clete warned him. "Don't stop."

Disorienting fog formed in front of them. As they pressed forward, Kyle began to hear accusatory voices saying, "You should have...Why didn't you...? What a dumb move you made there..." The voices started as low whispers, then became louder and more adamant. On and on, they continued. Kyle was shocked to realize the accusations transformed into small arrows, just as had happened with the enemies' darts back in the forest. They hit his helmet and slid down his chest.

With a whooshing sound, another arrow hit the ground in front of them with a thud. It had another note attached.

"Leave it!" Clete yelled. "We must carry on."

The fog darkened, and soon Kyle could no longer see Clete beside him. Panicking, he forgot about the guidebook and headed directly into the enemy's trap.

chapter twenty-four

THE CLOCK IN THE INTENSIVE CARE ROOM MARKED EVERY second loudly. Josh put his head in his hands, closed his eyes for a minute, then looked up at his wife.

"I'm not a religious man, Gayle," he admitted. "I know your parents go to church and have urged us to have their pastor come and pray for Kyle. I think it's time for that."

Gayle nodded, trying to keep her tears from flowing.

Later that day, the pastor stepped into the room. Both Josh and Gayle stood up to greet him.

"Thanks for coming, Reverend Chambers." Josh said, shaking his hand.

Gayle offered a slight smile. "Yes, thanks for coming."

"I'm glad to, and please call me Alan." The reverend turned his attention towards Kyle. He stood by the side of the bed as Josh and Gayle shared the details of Kyle's condition and how they were coping. Alan listened sympathetically. After a lull in the conversation, he said, "Shall we pray?"

Josh and Gayle sat back down and Alan took a seat beside Josh.

"Father in heaven," he began. "We cry out to You, thankful that You understand our heartaches and walk with us in the difficult places. We pray for Kyle's broken body lying here and ask for Your healing..."

By the time Reverend Chambers left the room ten minutes later, both Josh and Gayle felt hopeful.

chapter twenty-five

WITH ANOTHER WHOOSH, AN ARROW HIT KYLE IN THE LEG. HE dropped to his knees. *What? How can this be?*

"I got him!" a voice yelled triumphantly. "He's mine now!"

Kyle felt paralyzed as he heard the sound of the enemy running towards him.

"Clete, where are you?" Kyle gasped into the darkness. "I need you."

Instantly, Clete appeared over him. He pulled out a lit sword and pointed it at the oncoming enemy.

"No, you can't have him," Clete declared. "He belongs to the Powerful One."

"Oh yeah?" a gruff voice answered. "Where is the Powerful One now? He's abandoned him."

"He has not." A sharp pain burned in Kyle's leg. These words of belief were enough to lift the fog. To his surprise, he saw Clete duelling with the enemy. In one hand, the enemy fought with a sword, and in the other he swung the familiar chain of guilt.

Kyle lay on his stomach, the arrow protruding from his lower leg. Desperate and in pain, he remembered Mercy and Truth and how they had soothed his pain after the incident with the wolf.

"Powerful One," he called weakly. "Please send Mercy and Truth."

Then a strange thing happened: he heard a song in his head. *"Give thanks to the Lord, for he is good; his love endures forever."*[11] As he focused, he realized that the singing wasn't in his head; he was actually hearing a song. Mesmerized by the sound of the voices, he forgot about his pain.

He also realized that the clanging of the swords had stopped. Clete's enemy lay on the ground with his fingers cupped over his ears, Clete's sword over his exposed neck. Mercy and Truth ran to Kyle's side, singing. Truth took hold of the arrow in his leg and removed it, still singing, *"Give thanks to the Lord, for he is good; his love endures forever."* Mercy pressed gauze against Kyle's wound, stopping the bleeding as she applied her ointment. She then bound the leg tightly.

As Mercy and Truth worked on Kyle, Clete's enemy slipped a hand out of his fingered glove, grasping a dagger

---

[11] 1 Chronicles 16:34 (NIV).

hidden under his shirt. He thrust it up at Clete's heart. Sensing the movement, Clete twisted his sword, deflecting the lethal blow back into the attacker's throat, mortally wounding him.

"Are you okay, Clete?" Kyle asked once he was able to sit up. After observing the narrow escape, he was more concerned about Clete than himself.

"Yes, I am," Clete said simply, no doubt used to this type of fighting.

Mercy draped a jacket over Kyle's shoulders to keep him warm and help ward off shock.

"This jacket is a gift from the King." She then repeated the song, along with Truth, *"Give thanks to the Lord, for he is good; his love endures forever."*

As Kyle listened, a star shape appeared on the tunnel wall. A destination point!

"Clete, what does it say?" Kyle asked, pointing to the words written in the star.

Clete walked over to it and read aloud that the King would provide a *"garment of praise for the spirit of heaviness."*[12]

Mercy nodded. "Your jacket is a reminder, Kyle. Remember that the enemy doesn't like any singing that focuses on the King."

It's true, Kyle thought. *I feel so much better, especially after I heard that song.*

"Are you okay now? Can you walk?" Clete asked with concern. He handed Kyle his walking stick and encouraged him to stand.

---

[12] Isaiah 61:3 (KJV).

Kyle put his weight on the walking stick and limped slowly towards the end of the passage. Beyond it, he could see a grassy plain. The Powerful One would be waiting there.

"We had a close one, didn't we?" Kyle said to Clete as they made their way through the tunnel. "I want to check my heart symbol to see if it suffered any damage. The truth is, I feel some pain there. Those arrows were aimed straight at it!"

Kyle shuddered as he recalled their accuracy. He stopped, leaned his walking stick against the wall, and opened his guidebook. On the page, he saw an image of himself in the tunnel. Focusing on his heart symbol, he realized he was in grave danger. An arrow had pierced it!

He immediately recognized it had come from the voice that had told him the Powerful One wouldn't forgive him for his texts to George. He knew he had let that arrow sink into his thoughts. He had chosen to believe the lie. No wonder he felt a pain in his chest!

Kyle closed the guidebook and took up his walking stick.

When they arrived at the end of the tunnel, the Powerful One stood waiting for them.

Kyle hung his head. "I've got something to show you that I'm ashamed of. I'm struggling to believe that you've totally forgiven me for how I put down George." With that, Kyle opened his guidebook, revealing his wounded heart symbol. "I got hit in the tunnel. Can you remove it? I'm sorry that I believed the lie."

"Do you believe I can remove it?" the Powerful One asked searchingly.

Kyle nodded decisively. "Yes, I… I do."

As the Powerful One touched him, Kyle saw the wound on the man's hand.

"You've been made right in the King's eyes by believing, Kyle," the Powerful One said. "Remember, you are loved."

As Kyle listened, he felt the ache in his heart diminish. He then opened his guidebook to reveal the map. The Powerful One gestured to the mountain in the distance.

"That's your final destination, Kyle, but it is here where we must part. Remember, I'm not far from you. The King is expecting me, and I must go to him."

"I don't understand." Kyle shook his head, his eyes downcast.

"I know you don't," the Powerful One said. "One day, you will. First, I need to tell you about the plain before you. It's called the land of plenty. Look around you, Kyle."

He stretched out his arm, and unexpectedly Kyle saw masses of people he hadn't noticed before. They were spread out on either side of the path like a patchwork quilt. A huge spotlight highlighted one section at a time, so Kyle could observe what they were doing. In one section, people held cell phones and iPads. He watched as their thumbs moved over the keys, their eyes glued to the screens. In another section, people gathered around a mountain of food; they were too busy gorging themselves on delicacies to even speak. As the spotlight moved from section to section, Kyle could see that most weren't aware that they were trapped by materialism, sports, lying, greed, sex, money, and power.

However, some *were* aware. These people cried out to anyone who would listen, "Release us! Release us!"

Kyle caught his breath as the spotlight stopped on a bramble of thorny branches, just large enough to trap a person inside. A sign attached to it read "Fear of people." In fact, this was the very prison Clete had helped him escape from at the beginning of his journey.

"The truth will set them free just as it set you free," the Powerful One reminded him. "Will you speak the truth to them?"

Kyle's heart both stirred with desire and shrank back at the same time.

"What can *I* say?" Kyle asked. To his astonishment, a rainbow of colours shone from his guidebook, and he realized this was where he would find the words. "I will, and I cross my heart. But why do you have to go away?"

"Trust me," the Powerful One answered. "Clete is beside you and you have the guidebook. You are not alone. Remember to put your shield in front of you as you travel, for it will show that you believe in me." He watched Kyle tenderly, then turned and walked towards the mountain with Mercy and Truth alongside him.

chapter twenty-six

KYLE'S FAMILY CIRCLED HIS BED IN THE INTENSIVE CARE WARD. His head and leg were bandaged and his eyes had swollen shut. His face was beyond recognition. His crushed body fought to survive. Machines beeped regularly beside him, the tubes connecting him to them seeming like a maze of cooked spaghetti.

A week had passed and Kyle's eyelids began to twitch. Then the heart monitor flat-lined, triggering a piercing alarm.

Gayle cried out.

"The end is near," Josh said between gasps.

"We're prepared for this," the doctor announced as he reached for the paddles to stimulate Kyle's heart.

Josh and Gayle held each other's hands and prayed. A tear ran down Keith's cheek. Officer Cook waited quietly. The heart monitor beeped—

chapter twenty-seven

KYLE WATCHED THE PROMISED ONE WALK AWAY UNTIL HE disappeared over the crest of a hill.

He gave me a purpose, Kyle realized. Determined to fulfill this purpose, he stepped out with Clete beside him, positioning his shield in front of him. He took a few tentative steps along the trail.

His attention was captured by the people with the cell phones. Small circles of friends huddled together with their heads down. As he watched their expressions, he recognized that cyberbullying was going on. One person in every circle turned their faces away from the others as tears rolled down their cheeks. He observed them for a few moments and felt a pang of guilt.

"What can I say to them?" he said under his breath. "They're so focused on their texting. They're not even looking at me."

As he pondered the situation, something astonished him: on their wrists were iron shackles connected by a chain.

They have chains like I had. They need the Powerful One to set them free.

It wasn't going to be easy, though. Several guards patrolled nearby, dressed in heavy armour. Their swords were drawn, ready to challenge anyone who came close.

I wonder if there was a guard like that next to my original prison?

As Kyle stood on the path studying them, the guards eyed him menacingly. As if on cue, they ran towards him, swords in hand. Kyle remembered the Powerful One's words: "Faith is your shield, and that's why it's important to have it in front of you."

He raised his shield and struck them with his sword, driving them off. He ventured towards the now-unguarded group of texters. Even though they were oblivious to his presence, he asked, "Do you want to be free?"

One woman looked up and began laughing. "Free? What are you talking about? I'm free already!"

Most continued to text, yet some stopped to cast him an idle glance. Kyle pulled out his guidebook and opened it to the page that shone the brightest. There, he saw himself in the land of plenty, surrounded by these people chained at the wrists. As he stared, words appeared which he read in a strong voice: *"The truth will set you free."*

Without warning, a hand clamped over his mouth and pulled him backwards.

"Look at them," a deep voice whispered in his ear. "They don't care. Why are you speaking to them? They don't need to hear that."

Kyle pivoted to see who was behind him: a young man with a brimmed hat covering his eyes. The man's palm pressed harder over Kyle mouth. All Kyle could hear, besides the man's breath, was the tapping of keypads all around.

Kyle gripped the guidebook. With one swift blow, he elbowed the man, knocking him away. He held up the book and pointed its light directly into the man's eyes.

It was Mr. Fall Guy! His eyes squinted at the bright light.

"Stop that!" Mr. Fall Guy commanded. "Don't you see what you're doing to me?"

Kyle backed away, but he kept the light blazing into the man's eyes. The people around them stopped texting long enough to watch the unfolding drama.

Kyle began to repeat the words more forcefully: *"The truth will set you free."*

Mr. Fall Guy screeched horribly and jammed his fingers into his ears. "Stop," he demanded. "Stop. Stop. *Stop!*"

But his demand only made Kyle more determined to say the words over and over again. *"The truth will set you free. The truth will set you free!"*

As he repeated the words, more people looked in his

direction, their attention diverted from their devices. Mr. Fall Guy yelled all the louder, trying to distract them from the words of freedom.

A young woman in a black sweatshirt and tights suddenly burst into tears. Kyle recognized her; she had been involved in cyberbullying a girl at his school.

"It's hopeless," the girl wailed. "I can never be forgiven for hurting that girl. I saw her cry after she received my text." Tears spilled down her face behind dark sunglasses. "It's hopeless! What am I going to do?"

When Kyle looked in her direction, he was surprised to see Clete whispering something in her ear.

"I... I'd like to be set free," she said to him. She held up the chain connecting her wrists. "But my wrists are chained together! What can I do?"

"The truth shall set you free," Kyle repeated.

"What is truth?" she asked, turning to him. "Those words don't make any sense to me. How can you believe them? All I want is to be set free."

Kyle looked at the girl with blue eyes and dark curly hair. "Truth is in this guidebook. It's helped me on my journey. Trust the Powerful One to set you free. He's the only one who can give you a new heart. He can take your old one and bury it, if you give it to him. He'll give you words to build others up, not tear them down. He did it for me."

The girl gazed intently at him as if absorbing his words. She broke into a smile. "You know, I need the Powerful One's words. I believe he can set me free!"

Suddenly, a key appeared. Clete bent over to pick it up, then unlocked the chain that held her captive. The chain dropped with a clank.

"I'm free!" She jumped up and down, looking around at the other texters. "I'm no longer going to use my cell phone to put others down."

Some of the people watched her, amused. Others went on texting.

She ran up to Kyle. "Can I come with you?"

Kyle looked to Clete, who stood next to a teenager. From his expression, Kyle knew how to answer. "I think it would be better if you stayed and told these ones to become free like you."

Clete pulled another guidebook from his backpack and handed it to her. When the young woman opened the book, it lit up just as Kyle's had. Her face brightened.

"Yes!" she said enthusiastically. "I can stay, because I know what it's like to be chained! There's hope for them."

As Kyle observed her change of heart, he felt an urge to peek at his own guidebook, to check on the condition of his heart. As he did, an image of the Powerful One appeared on the page. In his outstretched hand, he held the symbol of Kyle's heart, shining with a brighter gleam than ever before. A message appeared under it: *"Trust in the Powerful One with all your heart, and do not rely on your own understanding."*[13]

---

[13] Proverbs 3:5–6 (NET, paraphrased).

Kyle smiled, realizing that the Powerful One was the only one he could trust to hold his heart, just as Lady Wisdom had said.

As Clete and Kyle continued towards the mountain, he again was captivated by all the people caught in traps like he had been. It was overwhelming.

He sat down on the grass and began recalling his journey to the castle. He remembered the King's words to guard his heart, and his admonishment to learn to live without guilt, fear, and shame. He recalled the forest and the hopelessness he'd felt when he tried to free himself using his own power. His thoughts then moved to the cursed tree where he had first met the Powerful One, a life-changing experience.

The guidebook lit up and he opened it to the page that shone the brightest. Surprisingly, he saw a picture of himself as a five-year-old listening to his mom sharing the Easter story. Overshadowing this scene was a cross, and then the image faded into the cursed tree he had once sat in. The Powerful One had died so that his heart could be free.

Only when I believed in the power of the cross could my heart truly be protected.

"Cross your heart," he pleaded with those around him. "Cross your heart!"

As he said these words, the King appeared before him, with the Powerful One on one side and Clete on the other. They smiled as the King extended his hand towards him.

"Well done, Kyle," the King said. "You now understand how to guard your heart. You have to keep the cross over it.

You taught the guidebook's truth, which sets the prisoners free. And you've remembered my words, that I am always with you. Well done, Kyle. You are ready to go home."

"But do I have to leave you?"

"Kyle, remember, I am always with you," the Powerful One emphasized.

Realizing the weight of responsibility he would have when he returned, but taking comfort in knowing he could do all things with the Powerful One who strengthened him, Kyle said simply, "Okay, I'm ready."